GAME ON!

Adapted by Tracey West

SCHOLASTIC INC.

New York Toronto London Auckland Sydney
Mexico City New Delhi Hong Kong Buenos Aires

ISBN-13: 978-0-545-01347-5
ISBN-10: 0-545-01347-X

© 1996 Kazuki Takahashi

Published by Scholastic Inc.
SCHOLASTIC and associated logos are trademarks and/or registered
trademarks of Scholastic Inc.

12 11 10 9 8 7 6 5 4 3 2 1   7 8 9 10 11/0

Printed in the U.S.A.   40

This edition first printing, January 2007

◆ CHAPTER ONE ◆

A BRUSH WITH GREATNESS

Some time in the future . . .

Jaden Yuki dashed down the busy streets of the city, pushing past startled passersby on their way to work. Jaden had some place to be, too — but it was a lot more exciting than some boring office.

"I got my deck, I got my gear, and I got about two minutes to get to the Duel Academy

Entrance Exams before they start," Jaden muttered to himself as he ran. Several blocks away the huge dome-shaped exam building rose above the cityscape. Even if he ran as fast as he could, he'd barely make it on time.

"Oh well," Jaden said, grinning. "At least since I'm not a student yet, they can't throw me in detention hall for being late!"

Jaden picked up his pace. The game of Duel Monsters had been his obsession for as long as he could remember. Now he had a chance to attend the Duel Academy — an elite training ground for the world's best young Duelists. Jaden knew it was his destiny to attend the academy, and nothing was going to stop him from going — especially not some slow-moving pedestrians.

"Excuse me! Comin' through!" Jaden cried, pushing past anyone in his way.

Then . . . *wham!* Jaden bumped into a tall man walking toward him. Jaden's Duel Disk and cards dropped to the sidewalk. He bent down and scrambled to pick them up.

"Sorry!" Jaden cried.

"You're a Duelist, aren't you?" the man asked.

"Yeah, I'm trying out at the academy today," Jaden replied. He looked up and pushed his long brown bangs out of his eyes. The man had striking purple eyes and spiky yellow hair. He looked familiar. But could it really be him?

"Hey, you're —" Jaden began. But before he could finish, the man held out a Duel Monsters card.

"Why don't you take this?" he asked. "Something just tells me it belongs with you."

Jaden looked at the card, which showed a small brown creature with big eyes and wings. A Winged Kuriboh. Not a superpowerful card, but a really useful one.

"Wow, for real?" Jaden asked.

"Good luck," the man said. Then he turned and walked away.

Jaden froze for a moment. He was sure that the man he had just encountered was Yugi Muto, the King of Games. The best Duelist in

Duel Monsters history. And he had just given Jaden a card!

"Thank you!" Jaden called out. "I'll make you proud!"

Jaden stared at the card for a moment. Then it hit him.

"Uh-oh!" he cried. "The exam! I can't be the *next* King of Games if I'm *late* to the games!"

Jaden sprinted across the street. He could take the long walkway that led to the arena's main entrance. Or he could try a shortcut. . . .

At the arena's front door, a Duel Academy official checked the list of applicants. He turned to two assistants standing nearby.

"Well, it looks like that's it," the official said. "Whoever hasn't shown up by now is out of luck."

Jaden heard the official's words as he climbed up the cement wall near the entrance and hoisted himself over the metal rail. The official and his assistants gaped in surprise to see the young man. Jaden smiled and landed safely on the platform in front of them.

"You can count Jaden Yuki as present, thank you!"

• CHAPTER TWO •

A SURPRISING OPPONENT

Jaden ran up the stairway to the top of the stands inside the arena. He could hear cheers and loud voices coming from the spectator area, and his heart began to pound with excitement. Every student who wanted to get into the academy had to duel the school's official examiners. Jaden would be dueling soon, and he couldn't wait.

He darted through the doorway into the

main arena. Rows and rows of seats circled four dueling fields marked on the floor in the center of the arena. The seats on the other side of the arena were filled with boys and girls in blue, red, and yellow uniforms — academy students. The kids on Jaden's side of the stands were dressed in street clothes. They were trying to get into the academy, just like Jaden. He walked up to a short boy with glasses and wild blue hair. The boy was leaning over the railing, watching a duel taking place on one of the fields below.

A confident-looking boy with brown hair faced an academy examiner, a man in a blue uniform and dark glasses. Two holographic images of Duel Monsters stood on the field in front of him.

The examiner sneered. "All right, new guy, multiple choice. You got two monsters staring you down. Do you, *A*, throw in the towel? *B*, beg for mercy? Or *C*, run home to momma?"

Jaden knew that the two monsters were tough opponents. Vorse Raider looked especially fierce with his giant battle-ax and horned helmet. But the young Duelist looked calm.

"I'll go with *D,* none of the above!" he replied.

"A trap?" The examiner sounded surprised.

"Exactly!" the Duelist responded. "With Ring of Destruction, I can destroy any monster

on the field that's in attack mode, and then we *both* take damage equal to that monster's attack points!"

The Duelist placed the Ring of Destruction on his Duel Disk, and a glowing metal ring floated over the field. The ring landed on Vorse Raider's neck and began to glow with red light. Vorse Raider roared in protest, and then *bam!* The monster exploded.

Jaden looked at the examiner's life points. Before the move, he had 1,300 life points, but after the attack, they were reduced to zero! The young Duelist had won!

The examiner grunted with reluctant respect. "Clever move, applicant. Welcome to the academy."

Bastion bowed. "Thank you, wise Proctor."

Jaden was impressed. Using Ring of Destruction was a move that needed to be perfectly calculated. It was a bold choice, and the Duelist had done it perfectly.

"Wow, that last guy really tore it up!" he remarked.

The boy with the glasses nodded. "Yeah, that's Bastion Misawa. They say he got the highest score on the written exam of all of us applicants."

"Wow!" Jaden replied. "I barely passed."

The boy nodded. "Me, too. My name's Syrus, by the way. Nice to meet you. I kind of have a thing where I get test anxiety. I don't know how I won my match!"

"So you're in?" Jaden asked.

"Yup," Syrus said, almost as if he didn't believe it himself.

"Congratulations!" Jaden cried. "I'll be in, too, as soon as I win *my* duel."

"You might have a problem," Syrus said nervously. "I think this was supposed to be the last duel."

Jaden frowned. He got in on time, didn't he? They'd have to let him duel.

He scanned the crowd. The academy officials were huddled together, talking. He wondered if they were deciding what to do with him.

Bastion Misawa walked up the stands and sat down in front of Jaden. He looked calm and composed in a white shirt and pants.

"Tight duel, Bastion!" Jaden told him.

Bastion looked up at Jaden. "Thank you," he replied.

Jaden grinned. "From the looks of it, you just might be the *second*-best Duelist here!"

Bastion raised an eyebrow in surprise. Before he could respond, a loud voice boomed over the sound system.

"Jaden Yuki, please report to Exam Field Four."

Jaden waved to Syrus and Bastion. "Go time!" he said. "Wish me luck, guys."

"Hey wait!" Bastion called out. "If I'm second-best, who's first?"

"Yours truly," Jaden replied. "It's what I'm best at!"

Bastion and Syrus stared after Jaden as he walked down to the exam field. A platform lifted him up to the battle area.

Jaden expected to face another examiner in a blue uniform and glasses, but the person standing across from him surprised him: The Duelist was tall, with yellow hair pulled back in a long ponytail, and a large nose. His blue suit was adorned with ruffly sleeves and a collar, like some kind of costume. Gold pads topped his shoulders, and a metal disk was strapped to his chest. His Duel Disk was long and curved, and gleamed silver under the arena lights.

"What's your name?" the examiner asked him.

Jaden realized he was staring and snapped out of his trance. "Uh, Jaden, Jaden Yuki!" he replied.

The examiner smiled, reminding Jaden of a crocodile about to gobble up a fish.

"Well, *uh,* Jaden Yuki," the examiner said. "I am Dr. Vellian Crowler — Department Chair of Techniques at Duel Academy!"

Up in the stands, Bastion and Syrus watched Jaden face off against Dr. Crowler.

"That Jaden is so sure of himself. I wonder if he's really that good," Syrus mused.

"He'd better be," Bastion said. "Dr. Crowler is a master Duelist. He knows every trick in the book."

Back on the floor, Jaden smiled confidently at Dr. Crowler.

"Wow, a department chair. I had no idea," he said. "From the way you were dressed, I thought you were some kind of weird academy mascot. Like a cheerleader."

Nervous laughs erupted from the stands. Nobody had ever talked to Dr. Crowler like that before — especially someone who wasn't even a student yet!

Dr. Crowler glared at Jaden. He pressed a button on the metal disk strapped to his vest.

"Duel Vest on!" he cried. A panel slid out of the disk, revealing his first five cards.

"Hey, that's pretty sweet, Teach!" Jaden said. "How do I get one of those cool Duel Blazers?"

"Oh, a lot of hard work and extremely high marks," Dr. Crowler replied. "Of course, you first have to get *in* to Duel Academy. And I will make certain that won't be happening!"

Dr. Crowler's challenge only made Jaden more anxious to battle. He loved a good competition.

Overhead, the scoreboards flashed the

life points for each player: 4,000. The field was ready.

"Let's duel!" Jason called out. He opened up his Duel Disk and dealt out the first five cards. Good. He held some of his favorites right in his hand.

"I'm gonna summon Elemental Hero Avian in defense mode," Jaden said. He placed the card on his Duel Disk, and an image of the card appeared on the field in front of him. The figure on the card looked like some kind of superhero,

with a green costume, wings, and feathers sprouting from the top of his head. The card's stats flashed on his Duel Disk: ATK 1,000/ DEF 1,000.

"I'll also throw down a facedown," Jaden added. He put another card facedown on the Duel Disk.

"All right!" Jaden cried. "Get your game on!"

Jaden waited, curious to see which cards Dr. Crowler would use. All of the examiners used special test decks so that they wouldn't have an unfair advantage against the students. That probably meant that Jaden would be familiar with whatever card came up.

Across the field, Dr. Crowler had other ideas. "I want to teach this little brat a lesson for being late," he muttered under his breath. "I'm using my own personal deck instead of a test deck. I'll fail him and send him home in no time."

Dr. Crowler called out to Jaden. "For this first move, I think I'll start nice and easy," he said. "I choose to play the spell card . . . Confiscation!"

Crowler revealed a card that showed a man running away with a treasure chest. Jaden had never seen it before.

"So what's it do?" he asked.

Crowler smiled, clearly enjoying his clever move. "It allows me to pay 1,000 life points for the chance to look at your hand — and toss one of your cards into the graveyard!"

Jaden watched as images of his cards floated in front of Dr. Crowler's face. It wasn't fair. Now Crowler could anticipate his moves. And which one of his cards was he going to lose?

"Oh yes, I remember some of these when I was a rookie," Dr. Crowler taunted. "Hmm, which one shall I banish? How about . . . Monster Reborn to the graveyard!"

Jaden tried to keep his cool. Monster Reborn was a great card. It had helped him win a lot of duels.

"Next, I'll lay two of my cards down on the

field," Dr. Crowler said, putting the cards on his Duel Disk. The professor sounded very cheerful.

Crowler must be up to something, Jaden guessed. But what?

"And last but not least, I'll play Heavy Storm!" Crowler cried, placing a card faceup. A strong wind swirled on the field. "This spell card destroys every other spell and trap card that's out on the field."

The wind blew stronger, carrying away the trap card that Jaden had facedown on the field — but it also blew away Dr. Crowler's cards.

"Whoopsie! Did you forget you had two trap cards out on the field yourself?" Jaden asked him.

But Dr. Crowler just giggled, pleased with himself. Anxious whispers came from the crowd.

"What's happening?" Jaden asked, nervous. Dr. Crowler couldn't be using a standard test deck — he had never seen *any* of these cards! "Could somebody tell me what's going on?"

Up in the stands, Bastion explained things to Syrus. "The two trap cards Dr. Crowler had on the field were called Statue of the Wicked," he said. "It's a special trap that creates a vicious Token monster when destroyed. That's why he played Heavy Storm — to activate the trap."

As Bastion spoke, two serpentlike monsters with shimmering gold bodies rose on the field. They both roared, revealing sharp fangs, and they scratched at the air with their long, sharp claws.

Jaden didn't look scared. Once you lost confidence in a duel, it was game over.

"Ready for your next lesson?" Dr. Crowler asked Jaden.

Jaden smiled confidently. "You bet! I can't remember the last time learning was this much fun!"

Jaden's confidence disappointed Crowler. "Yes, well, I'm quite an excellent teacher," he snarled. "And now, I sacrifice my two Wicked Tokens!"

The monsters on the field roared and thrashed as they burst into flame.

"I summon Ancient Gear Golem!" Dr. Crowler cried.

Everyone in the stands gasped in surprise. When Crowler played the card, a giant stone monster rose from the floor of the field. It looked like a huge robot made of boulders. An astounding 3,000 attack points flashed on the scoreboard.

• CHAPTER FOUR •

BATTLING A LEGEND

Jaden stared up at the huge monster. How on earth was he supposed to beat that? He could just see his chances of going to Duel Academy swirling right down the drain. . . .

"Now, now," Dr. Crowler said. "I hope you're not too scared of my legendary Ancient Gear Golem!"

Don't let 'em see you sweat, Jaden. "Aw,

no way!" he replied. "I've always wanted to take one on!"

Amazed cries burst from the stands. Bastion and Syrus looked at each other, stunned. Jaden was staring down the legendary monster like he didn't have a care in the world.

"Either Jaden's brave or he's nuts!" Syrus said.

Dr. Crowler chuckled. "Golem, attack!" he cried. "Mechanized Melee!"

On the field, the huge stone monster

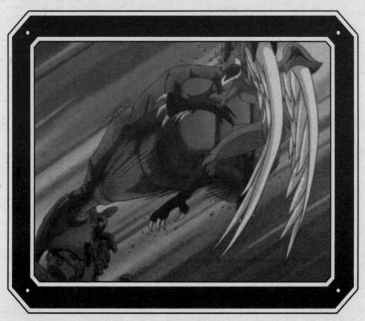

pummeled Jaden's Elemental Hero Avian with a massive stone fist. The hero reeled from the blow, and then vanished from the field.

"Aw, Jaden's monster didn't stand a chance!" Syrus cried. "His defense points were way too low. This isn't looking good."

Bastion nodded. "And it's about to get a lot worse. When that Ancient Gear Golem attacks a monster in defense mode, the difference between its attack points and the defending monster's defense points gets dealt to the opponent as damage."

Syrus gasped. "But that would mean . . . Jaden's life points are gonna take a hit!"

The holographic monster raised its fist and passed it right through Jaden's body. Jaden's 4,000 life points dropped to 2,000.

"Don't feel bad," Crowler said breezily. "This is the top dueling school in the country. Not everyone is cut out to be —"

Crowler stopped, surprised. Jaden was actually laughing!

"Boy, I really want to come to your school

now, Teach," he said. "You really know your stuff!"

Dr. Crowler frowned, frustrated. "Can't he take a hint?" he muttered under his breath. "He will not be allowed to pass this exam. And he certainly won't be permitted to make a mockery of my deck!"

The professor trembled with rage. He was definitely angry, but also looked impressed.

Then Jaden heard a faint, echoing whistle. It was coming from his deck! He quickly dealt his next card.

The Winged Kuriboh that Yugi had given him looked up at him.

"Oh, it's you!" Jaden said. He remembered Yugi's words. *Something just tells me it belongs with you.*

"Something's starting to tell me that, too," Jaden said.

The Winged Kuriboh on the card seemed to wink at him.

"I'll take that as a sign to play you," Jaden said. He held up the card.

"I summon Winged Kuriboh in defense mode!"

The little brown monster appeared on the field in front of Jaden.

"And I'll place another card facedown," Jaden said. "Not bad, huh, Teach?"

Dr. Crowler shook his head. "Not bad, but you must understand, I'm a master technician," he said. "A Kuriboh to me is rather ordinary. Even one with wings is no match for Ancient Gear Golem. It's a textbook mistake. Don't feel bad."

Jaden just grinned back at him.

"Now let's proceed," Crowler said. "Ancient Gear Golem — attack that Kuriboh with Mechanized Melee!"

The huge stone monster pounded the little Kuriboh. It vanished from the field with a whimper.

"Sorry, Winged Kuriboh," Jaden whispered.

Crowler looked at his Duel Disk. Jaden's life points were still at 2,000.

"Check your gear," he told Jaden. "Your life points haven't changed."

"My gear's fine," Jaden replied. "On the turn Winged Kuriboh is destroyed, I sustain zero damage!"

Crowler looked surprised. Jaden had made a move that even the professor didn't know about.

"Fine," Dr. Crowler huffed. "I guess your lame little monster saved you there."

"Hey, slow down there, Teach," Jaden

protested. "You may have beat him, but that doesn't give you the right to call him lame."

"Oh yes," Dr. Crowler said, his voice dripping with sarcasm. "I forget how attached you new Duelists get to your monsters. I'm sorry."

Jaden's brown eyes glittered. This was the moment he'd been waiting for.

"You *should* be sorry, Teach," he replied. "Because by attacking my Winged Kuriboh, you set off a trap card!"

• CHAPTER FIVE •

JADEN'S TRAP

"It's one of my favorite trap cards," Jaden told a stunned Crowler. "Hero Signal!"

As Jaden turned over the card, a bright line shone on the arena ceiling. A letter *H* shone in the center of the beam.

"That brings out my second elemental hero, Burstinatrix!"

Dr. Crowler cringed as Jaden put the card faceup. Burstinatrix wore a red hero's uniform, red eye mask, and a gold helmet on her head. Long, black wings streamed from her head, looking like hair.

"All right, Winged Kuriboh," Jaden whispered. "This one's gonna be for you."

Jaden turned up another card. "Now I'm going to bring back Avian to my hand with a spell card, Warrior Returning Alive!"

The green-suited Elemental Hero Avian appeared on the field next to Burstinatrix.

Dr. Crowler looked relieved. "You've made

another amateur mistake," he said. He turned to the crowd. "Would anyone like to tell me what our little friend did wrong here?"

"Actually, I wasn't done yet," Jaden interrupted him. "I know my two heroes aren't very powerful by themselves. But if I can form them together, that's another story. And I have just the card to unite them!"

Jaden held out one more card. "Polymerization! Join Avian and Burstinatrix! Fusion Summon!"

The two Hero monsters rose from the field and began to swirl in a whirlwind of glowing light. When the light faded, a new monster had formed: a huge red and green creature with wings. One of his arms was red and ended in a fierce dragon's head. A spiky red dragon's tail thrashed around the field. Huge white wings sprouted from his back, and a green and red mask covered his face — and 2,100 attack points flashed on Jaden's Duel Disk.

The crowd gasped. Jaden had summoned a pretty powerful monster.

"There he is — Elemental Hero Flame Wingman!" Jaden announced. "I hope your Gear Golem is ready for a clash of the titans!"

Wingman grunted, ready for battle.

"So, Teach, what do you think?" Jaden asked.

"I think you're dueling very well for an amateur," Dr. Crowler said. "But next time, try playing a monster that has more attack points than what's already out."

"What does he mean?" Syrus asked Bastion.

"He means that Wingman's 2,100 attack points are no match for his Golem's 3,000," Bastion explained. "It's a shame, too, because when the Wingman destroys a monster, *that* monster's attack points are dealt as damage to his owner."

"You mean they're deducted right out of his life points?" Syrus asked. That would really hurt Crowler. But it didn't matter — there was no way Wingman could destroy Golem with only 2,100 attack points. "Too bad. That would have been a great way for Jaden to turn things around."

"Well, if your friend's as good as he says he is, he might still find a way," Bastion said thoughtfully.

"Wow!" Syrus said. "Did we really seem like friends?"

Back on the field, Crowler was growing impatient. "Let's get this over with, young man. I am a busy man! Are you done yet?"

"Of course I'm not done yet!" Jaden replied. "I knew my Wingman had fewer attack points than your Golem. That's why I have this."

Jaden turned up another card. "Skyscraper! Go!"

A tall building began to rise on the field, and it was followed by more tall buildings. The Skyscraper card was a field card, trans-forming the dueling field into a cityscape. Ancient Gear Golem stomped among the buildings.

Wingman jumped on top of the first build-ing, which kept growing until it towered over the arena. Wingman looked down over the field.

"All right, Flame Wingman!" Jaden cried. "Show them what kind of hero you are and attack Ancient Gear Golem!"

Dr. Crowler simply scowled. "Fine with me," he said. "That silly little Skyscraper field card hasn't lowered my Golem's attack level at all!"

"You know what, Teach, you're right,"

Jaden replied. "This Skyscraper field hasn't lowered your Golem's attack points at all. What it's done is raise the attack points of Elemental Hero Wingman by one thousand!"

On the Duel Disk, Wingman's attack points jumped to 3,100.

"Wait! Time out!" Crowler cried helplessly.

"Wingman, go!" Jaden cried. "Skydive Scorcher!"

A ball of red-hot flame enveloped

Wingman's body. He dove down from the tall tower, aimed at Ancient Gear Golem.

Slam! Wingman crashed into the stone monster. A white-hot fireball bubbled up from the floor of the field, followed by a thundering explosion. Pieces of the tall buildings rained down on the field.

When the dust cleared, Golem collapsed — right onto a frantic Dr. Crowler!

"He was my very best card!" Dr. Crowler whimpered.

"And because of Wingman's superpower, the attack points of your Golem are dealt straight to your life points!" Jaden added. "Sweet, huh?"

"No way!" the professor cried. A pained look crossed his face as he watched his life points dwindle down to zero.

"That's game," Jaden said. "So I guess I passed the test, huh, Teach?"

"Impossible!" Dr. Crowler groaned. "There's no way this delinquent could defeat me!"

Jaden raced back up into the stands. Syrus ran to greet him.

"Way to go, Jaden," he said.

"Nice," Bastion said, nodding from his seat. "I could use a little competition."

Jaden jumped up in the air and spun around. "I made the academy! I'm in! I'm in!"

Jaden stopped for a minute and took out his cards. His dream had come true — but he couldn't have done it without his Duel Monsters. He owed a lot to one monster, especially.

"We're *both* in," he said quietly, looking at the Winged Kuriboh. "And from here on out, you and I will be partners."

The Winged Kuriboh winked in reply.

‹ CHAPTER SIX ›

DUEL ACADEMY, DAY ONE!

"Attention, Duel Academy students. If you look outside the windows, you'll see your new home away from home!"

The pilot's announcement blared through the helicopter filled with new Duel Academy students. Jaden jumped from his seat and scrambled over to the window to get a better view.

"I know you're excited, but don't shove!" the pilot scolded.

Jaden took in the sight below him: a lush green island crowned with a towering volcano. Several large buildings dotted the landscape.

That's where I'm gonna live, Jaden thought, excitement growing inside him. *It's my next stop on the way to becoming King of Games!*

"Fasten your seat belts and bring your seats back to an upright position," the pilot

said. "We're going to land. Next stop: Academy Island!"

When the helicopter landed, the new students were herded into the largest building on the island. Jaden saw that they faced a large screen on which the pleasant face of a bald man with a beard suddenly appeared.

"Good morning and welcome, my students," the man said. "I'm Chancellor Sheppard, the headmaster here, and you are the best and brightest young Duelists in the world!"

Some of the students clapped, but Jaden tapped his foot impatiently. When were they going to get to duel?

"Now please — get yourselves settled in your assigned dorms," the headmaster said. "I think you'll find them quite comfortable. Depending on how you ranked, of course."

The screen dimmed, and the students were led into another room. A few minutes later, Jaden emerged wearing a new red jacket and sat down next to Syrus.

"Well, I don't know about you, but it looks like I'm in the Slifer Red Dorm," Jaden boasted.

"That's cool!" Syrus said, excited. "Same with me!"

Just then, Bastion walked past. Jaden called out to him. "You in Red, too?"

Bastion looked down at his yellow jacket. "Well, now let's see here — yellow sleeves, yellow buttons . . . I don't think so."

Jaden realized that Syrus was wearing a red jacket, too.

"I get it. That's why Syrus and I are both in red," he said.

Bastion shook his head. "Please don't tell me you only just figured that out now," he said.

"So what?" Jaden shrugged. "Ever think I'm color blind?"

"Well, no I didn't," Bastion said. "Are you color blind?"

"Nope, but I could've been!" Jaden joked. "See you around the dorms!"

"I doubt that," Bastion said. He nodded his head toward the left. "Your dorm's over there."

Jaden looked to the left. Bastion pointed toward a ramshackle, two-story building near the beach. Jaden nodded to Syrus, and the two boys walked to the dorm. As they got closer, they saw that the wood was rotting in places, and paint had peeled from the walls long ago.

"This isn't a dorm," Syrus complained as they walked the rickety steps to the second floor. "It's like an outhouse with a deck."

"You kidding me?" Jaden said. Nearby, a white sandy beach led to the beautiful blue water. "Check out the view! This place is great."

Jaden entered the hallway and walked from door to door. "This one's our room," he announced, pushing open the door.

The boys gazed at the space, which was bare except for metal bunk beds, two desks with computers, and a small stove and sink.

"It's kind of small, huh?" Syrus asked.

"Hey, you're a small guy!" Jaden said. "Anyway, this will make a sweet pad for our first year here."

"Yeah, it's kind of weird, isn't it?" Syrus asked, pushing up his glasses. "First we met at the Entrance Exams, and now we're room-mates."

Syrus gazed off into the distance. "Maybe

we were connected in some past life. Like, you were an Egyptian Pharaoh, and I was the Guardian Seto."

Jaden made a face. "No offense, but that's just lame."

"Well, it could be true," Syrus said.

"Forget it," Jaden said. "They broke the mold when they made the two of us."

Syrus sighed. "Yeah — for different reasons."

Jaden shook his head. "Sy, we're going to have to work on that confidence," he said. "But first, let's work on this pad!"

Jaden threw open the closed curtains. Sunlight streamed through the windows.

"Hey, those were closed for a reason!" an angry voice boomed.

Jaden and Syrus jumped. The voice was coming from the top bunk.

"Sorry, we didn't see you up there," Jaden said.

"Well, can you see me now?"

The blanket on the top bunk flew off to reveal a huge boy with a mean-looking face.

"Aaaaaaah!" Jaden and Syrus screamed.

CHAPTER SEVEN
CHAZZ'S CHALLENGE

"Who are you, and what are you doing in my room?" the large boy bellowed.

"My name's Jaden Yuki," Jaden said.

"And I'm Syrus," Syrus added.

"Looks like we're you're new roommates," Jaden said.

The boy groaned and rolled over. "Yeah, you're new all right," he said. "Let me tell you how things work around here."

"You mean like when parents' weekend is going to be?" Syrus asked.

"Duh, like how the whole color thing works," the boy said. "That's more important than anything."

He rolled over again and stared at the ceiling.

"You got three different kinds of students here," he began. "Obelisk Blue students, Ra Yellow students, and Slifer Red students."

Jaden nodded. Each group was named after a different Egyptian God card.

"Now, the Blues are the highest ranked students," the boy continued. "Some kids are Blue because of grades, but other kids are Blue 'cause they got money or know somebody important. The Yellows are the second highest. Mostly younger students with lots of potential." He paused. "Then there's us. The Red wonders."

"Wonders, huh? That's a cool name!" Syrus said.

"Wonders, as in, I wonder how those flunkies got this far!" the boy finished. Syrus frowned. "Sorry, but we're the bottom of the battle here. Duelin' duds. I'm Chumley, by the way."

Syrus turned away and walked out of the room, a dismal look on his face. Jaden followed him. The boys walked down the steps in silence and headed back toward the main campus.

"Aw, come on, Syrus. Don't be depressed!" Jaden pleaded.

"But Chumley said we Reds are the worst!" Syrus moaned.

Jaden turned and walked backward, facing Syrus. "Forget that, man. Red's a sweet color! Think about it. Where do you think the term 'red hot' comes from? From *red*, baby!"

This seemed to cheer up Syrus a bit.

"Besides, the year hasn't even started yet, so how can we be the worst?" Jaden pointed out.

"Yeah, you're right, Jaden!" Syrus cried. He got a dreamy look in his eyes. "Red is for 'red hot!' Scorching! Dangerous! Like a fiery furnace! Or . . . a really big bottle of salsa dip!"

Jaden turned and began to run ahead.

"Wait! I'm not a dip!" Syrus cried. "Where are you going?"

Syrus dashed ahead and caught up to Jaden. He was headed toward a fancy building with tall marble pillars lining the center courtyard.

"There's some kind of duel action going on in there," Jaden said.

"How do you know?" Syrus asked.

"I just know," Jaden said. It was hard to explain. It was like dueling was in his blood. If there was a duel going on, Jaden could feel it.

Jaden raced through the courtyard and pushed through two large double doors. He stepped into a dome-shaped duel arena. Syrus walked up next to him.

Jaden let out a low whistle. "Wow!" he cried. "This is the sweetest dueling arena I've ever seen!"

"No kidding," Syrus said. "It looks completely state-of-the-art."

A large dueling field took up the center of the arena. Neat green bleachers surrounded the room, and gleaming metal panels shone on the walls.

"I bet it would be amazing to duel here," Syrus said.

Jaden turned to him, his eyes gleaming.

"Well, let's find out!" He couldn't wait to duel in this place.

"Do you think we're allowed?" Syrus asked nervously.

"Sure we're allowed," Jaden said. "We're students here, and this is our campus, right?"

"Wrong!" a voice said. "This is the Obelisk Blue's campus!"

Jaden and Syrus turned to see two boys in blue uniforms walk toward them. One boy had dark hair and wore glasses; the other had light, spiky hair.

"You Slifer Red rejects aren't welcome here. Got that?" the spiky-haired boy said.

"This arena's our turf," said the other boy.

Syrus was so nervous that he began to sweat and his glasses fogged up. "Sorry. We were just looking around. But we'll leave now. Right, Jaden?"

But Jaden remained cool. "Nah. We don't have to leave. Not so long as one of you guys agrees to duel me!" He didn't care whom he faced off against — just as long as he got to duel.

A look of realization came across the face of the boy with glasses. "Hey, you're that kid!"

The other boy recognized Jaden, too. "Hey, Chazz!" he called up to the stands. "It's that kid who beat Dr. Crowler!"

Jaden looked up to see another boy in a blue uniform standing a few rows above them. He had dark eyes, and his black hair rose in severe spikes all over his head. He looked at Jaden suspiciously.

"Hey, what's up," Jaden said. "My name's Jaden. He called you Chuzz or something, right?"

The boy with the glasses stepped right up to Jaden's face. "His name's Chazz Princeton, and he was the number-one Duelist back at Duel Prep School. So you make sure you pay him the proper respect, all right?"

"Yeah, he's going to be the future King of Games," the other boy added.

"Impossible," Jaden said. "I'm gonna be the next King of Games!"

The two boys laughed. "A Slifer slacker as King of Games? That'll be the day!"

But Chazz wasn't laughing. "Can it, you two!" he barked. "Maybe the new kid's right."

"What do you mean, Chazz?" asked the boy with glasses.

"He did beat Crowler and that legendary

monster of his," Chazz said. "I suppose it takes skill to pull that off."

"Got that right!" Jaden said.

"Or was it luck? I say we find out right now!" Chazz challenged him.

"Bring it!" Jaden cried.

"This sure is a motley crew."

The boys turned to see a girl walk into the arena. She had long, honey-colored hair and big, light brown eyes. She wore a white shirt with blue trim and a short blue skirt.

"Hey, Alexis," Chazz said. "Have you come to watch me wipe the floor with my new little friend here? It'll be a short duel, but an entertaining one for sure."

Jaden's finger's itched to grab his Duel Disk. He couldn't wait to duel.

"I'm here to remind you about the Obelisk welcome dinner. You're late," Alexis scolded.

Chazz and his two friends walked out of the arena. Jaden felt cheated. He wanted to teach that guy a thing or two!

Alexis turned to him. "Sorry if Chazz

rubbed you the wrong way. All of us Obelisks aren't like that. He can be a jerk — especially with Slifers."

Jaden shrugged. "It's no big deal," he said. "Guys like him don't bother me at all. Besides, I would have beaten him in one turn!"

Syrus shook his head. "We're going to have to work on that overconfidence."

"Okay, two turns," Jaden relented. "Maybe two and a half."

Alexis laughed. "You know, the Slifer welcome dinner's about to start, too. You'd better get back to your dorm."

"Right!" Jaden said. He turned and ran out of the arena. Then he paused and turned. "Hey, what was your name again?"

"Alexis Rhodes," the girl replied.

"My name's Jaden," Jaden told her. "See you around!" He broke into a run once again.

Syrus tried to keep up. "You know, you could have introduced me. . . ."

Jaden kept running. He had a bunch of energy in him that was just waiting to break out into a duel. He had already been at Duel Academy one whole day, and he hadn't dueled once!

CHAPTER EIGHT

GAME ON!

Across the Duel Academy campus, each of the dorms began its welcome dinner.

In Obelisk Blue, tuxedoed waiters passed out cheese balls to students in blue uniforms.

In Ra Yellow, students sat around a long table piled high with plates of food. Candles glimmered in the dim light as their headmaster gave a speech.

In Slifer Red, the students sat in dilapidated

wooden chairs around small folding tables. On each table was one bowl of rice and one plate of fish. A yellow cat dozed comfortably on top of an empty table in the front of the room.

Most of the Red students looked miserable.

"This is our fancy welcome dinner?" one complained.

"Forget that. Check out our headmaster. It's a cat!" joked another.

The cat yawned and hopped off the table. Behind him, a curtain opened, and a tall young man stepped out. He had long, dark hair, wire-rimmed glasses, and a friendly smile.

"Hello, children," the man said. "I am your headmaster, Professor Banner. Now, before we eat, I'd like you each to tell us something about your —"

"Mmmmm! This stuff's good!" Jaden stuffed another forkful of rice and fish into his mouth.

Syrus nudged him, mortified. "Jaden, we're supposed to say something about our-selves!"

"How about this, then? I'm starving!" Jaden joked.

Professor Banner walked to Jaden's table. Syrus trembled nervously. But Professor Banner smiled.

"Well, since some of us don't feel like waiting, let's eat!"

Later, Jaden sat on the floor of his room with his back against the wall, feeling content.

The food really was good. He rubbed his belly. "Man, I'm stuffed!" he said. "Professor Banner sure can cook."

Syrus poured hot tea into three mugs on a small tray. He carried the tray over to Jaden. "Yeah, and he seems like a pretty nice guy, too."

"You're right," Jaden said, taking the tea. "Thanks!"

Syrus raised a cup of tea to the top bunk. "Hey, Chumley, want some tea?"

"Did I say I was thirsty?" Chumley growled.

Syrus quickly backed up.

"Hey, he just asked if you wanted some tea," Jaden said. "You don't have to snap at him."

"That's okay," Syrus sighed. "I'm used to it."

"Don't you know that tea makes you wet the bed?" Chumley said grumpily. "Not that I do it. Or ever did it. I mean — whatever! I'm trying to sleep." He rolled over and pulled the covers over his head.

Jaden heard a beeping sound. He reached into his pocket and pulled out his Duel Academy communication device. A tiny envelope flew across the screen. Then Chazz's face appeared.

"Hey, Slifer slacker. Don't think you're off the hook," Chazz said. "It's on tonight at midnight. Oh, and why don't we make it interesting? Whoever wins gets the loser's best card!"

When the message ended, the screen went blank.

"Cool!" Jaden said. "Guess I'll get to duel at that arena after all."

Chumley stuck his head out from under his blankets. "If that's Chazz you're dueling, all you got is trouble."

Syrus looked nervous. "I'm not so sure it's a good idea, Jaden."

Jaden shrugged. "Good or bad, when

someone challenges you to a duel, you gotta step up! There's no choice!"

Just before midnight, Jaden and Syrus walked through the campus to the Obelisk Blue dorm. They stepped inside the arena to find Chazz and his two friends waiting in the stands.

"Well, well, well," Chazz said. "He shows."

"You better believe it," Jaden said. "There's no way I was gonna miss this!"

Chazz stepped up to Jaden and looked him in the eyes. "It's time to find out if you beating Dr. Crowler was a fluke or a fact."

Jaden's eyes narrowed. "Yeah, well, we're going to find out something else, too," he said. "Like which one of the two of us is really going to become the next King of Games!"

Chazz scowled. "Whatever," he said. "Just make sure you have your best card ready to hand over when you lose."

Jaden nodded. "You, too. Game on!"

• CHAPTER NINE •

OUT OF CONTROL!

Jaden and Chazz faced off across the dueling field. Both boys started out with 4,000 life points. Chazz fanned out his Duel Disk and held up five cards.

"All right, slacker," he began. "For my first move, I'll summon Reborn Zombie in defense mode."

Chazz put the card on his Duel Disk, and an image of the monster appeared on the field — a creepy corpse with ragged clothes covering a bony body. Reborn Zombie let out a loud battle roar.

"I'll also place one card facedown," Chazz said.

Jaden raised an eyebrow. "I guess that's one way to start a duel," he said. "But I'm going to start a little bigger."

Jaden looked at the five cards in his hand. Winged Kuriboh called out to him, and leaned out of the deck.

"Hey! Good to see you!" Jaden told the monster. "Maybe I'll use you later. But now, I'll play Polymerization!"

He put the card on his Duel Disk. Then he held up two more cards.

"That'll fuse Elemental Hero Avian and Burstinatrix!" Jaden cried.

The two monsters transformed on the field, forming the tall red and green hero with the dragon tail and wings.

"Bringing out Elemental Hero Flame Wingman in attack mode!" he said triumphantly. Jaden was proud of his move. Wingman had defeated Dr. Crowler — maybe he would defeat Chazz in one turn after all!

"I told you I'd start big, didn't I?" Jaden asked confidently.

But Chazz was smiling calmly. "I was hoping you would."

"Why's that?" Jaden asked. Chazz was up to something.

"Because that card I just played facedown was a trap, slacker!" Chazz cried with glee. "A

trap that *you've* set off. Cthonian Polymer, do your stuff!"

Syrus watched from the sidelines, confused. "What's Cthonian Polymer's stuff?" he asked.

Alexis walked up behind Syrus. "I had a feeling I'd find you guys here," she said. "Cthonian Polymer's a nasty trap. It allows you to take control of your opponent's Fusion monster by sacrificing one of your own creatures."

Syrus processed this. Wingman was a fusion of Avian and Burstinatrix. That meant . . . "Jaden just summoned a Fusion monster!"

Chazz turned over the trap card with a flourish.

"I sacrifice Reborn Zombie to gain control of your Wingman!" he cried.

Reborn Zombie wailed and disappeared from the field. Jaden watched in horror as Wingman — his strongest monster — vanished

from his side of the field and appeared on Chazz's side!

"No way!" Jaden cried.

How was he going to beat Chazz without his Wingman?

• CHAPTER TEN •

LOW ON LIFE POINTS . . .

"You're so predictable, Jaden," Chazz said. "I saw you use Wingman against Dr. Crowler at the exam. I was sure you would use him early in the duel. And I was right, as always."

Strategies raced through Jaden's mind. "Still, that Wingman was a special summon," he said. "That means I can summon another monster on my turn."

Chazz smirked. "Go ahead, Slifer slacker," he told himself. "Play another monster. After all, I haven't forgotten Flame Wingman's super-power."

Jaden continued his move. "I summon Elemental Hero Clayman in defense mode!"

He placed the card on his Duel Disk, and a sturdy gray monster appeared on the field. He had a round body and massive arms and legs that looked like giant blocks of clay.

"All set," Jaden said.

"Yeah! All set to get knocked down," Chazz taunted. He held up a new card. "Rise, Cthonian Soldier!"

A muscled warrior wearing an armored vest and helmet appeared on the field. His attack points flashed: 1,200.

"And now, Flame Wingman, attack with Skydive Scorcher!"

Flames burst from Wingman's body, and he flew across the field, slamming into Clayman. The strong monster reeled from the attack, and then vanished from the field. Jaden cringed.

"And now, thanks to Wingman's super-power, your life points take damage equal to your destroyed monster's attack points!" Chazz cried.

Wingman's dragon arm reached out toward Jaden, and the dragon's huge mouth opened up and began to suck the life points out of Jaden. His points dropped from 4,000 to 3,200. Jaden felt like he had been punched in the gut. His own attack was being used against him.

"But don't think I'm done yet, slacker!" Chazz said. "Cthonian Soldier! Attack! Windstorm Slash!"

With no monster on the field to defend Jaden, the soldier came right for him, landing a glancing blow that swept Jaden off his feet. All of Cthonian Soldier's attack points were taken from Jaden's life points. They plummeted from 3,200 to 2,000.

Chazz looked smug. "Are you starting to know your place at the academy yet? You might have been somebody big back home, but here in the big leagues, you're nothing but a pathetic amateur, Slifer slime!"

Chazz held up another card. "I'll end my turn with a facedown card. Your turn, slacker."

Jaden had lowered his head, and Chazz heard him make strangled sounds across the field.

"Oh, what's wrong, baby? Are you crying?" Chazz teased.

Jaden raised his head — and he was laughing!

"This is too fun!" he cried. Chazz looked stunned.

"It's just what I came for," Jaden continued. "The trash talking, the action, it's all so great!"

Jaden held up his next card. "I summon Elemental Hero Sparkman!"

A monster that looked like a superhero with a body made of metal appeared on the field. Jaden's Duel Disk flashed 1,600 attack points.

"Sparkman, attack with Static Shockwave!" Jaden called out.

Waves of electric energy radiated from Sparkman. They slammed into Chazz's Cthonian Soldier. The monster vanished with a cry — and Chazz's life points dropped from 4,000 to 3,600.

"Don't you know anything, slacker?" Chazz asked. "When Cthonian Soldier is destroyed, you receive the same amount of damage to your life points as I do. The difference is — you hardly have any to spare!"

Jaden watched as his life points dropped from 2,000 to 1,600.

"It's just a matter of time, slacker!" Chazz cried out. "The best card in your deck is going to be mine!"

"This isn't over yet!" Jaden shot back. "I throw a facedown!"

Chazz shook his head. "You can play what you like. My next attack is going to finish off your life points. And that attack's coming right now! Go, Flame Wingman!"

Wingman sprang into action. Flames leapt from his body.

"Not so fast!" Jaden cried, holding up his hand. "That was a trap card I just threw!"

"A trap?" Chazz didn't look so confident now.

Jaden overturned the card. It pictured a glowing blue mirror.

On the sidelines, Syrus gasped. "He's using Mirror Gate!"

Alexis smiled. "Then Jaden is still in this

duel after all," she said. "Mirror Gate makes two monsters in a battle switch the sides they're on."

In a flash, Sparkman and Wingman switched places on the field. Now Wingman stood on Jaden's side, facing Chazz and Sparkman.

"Yeah! Go, Wingman!" Jaden cheered.

Wingman advanced toward Sparkman, and the two heroes flew above the field, locking arms. Bolts of jolting electricity bounced around the field as the two heroes met, but the shiny metal hero was no match for Wingman's attack points. Sparkman exploded on the field.

"Nooooooo!" Chazz wailed.

"It's just like you told me," Jaden said. "Don't forget my Wingman's superpower. You take damage equal to the attack points of your destroyed monster!"

Chazz whined as his life points dwindled from 3,600 to 1,500 in one shot.

"All right!" Syrus cheered.

"Nice moves, Jaden!" Alexis called out.

Chazz scowled. "More like lucky moves if you ask me, you Slifer slacker." He took a new card from his deck. "I activate Cthonian Blast!"

A confident grin returned to Chazz's face. "Now, since you destroyed one of my monsters, I can destroy one of yours. And you take damage equal to half of its attack points!"

Flame Wingman vanished from the field. Then Jaden's life points dropped from 1,600 to 550.

"Now I activate the trap card Call of the

Haunted!" Chazz cried. "It lets me select one monster card and summon it back to the field in attack mode. Rise, Cthonian Soldier, Infernal Warrior!"

Once again, Chazz's armored soldier appeared on the field.

"But he won't be staying on the field for long," Chazz said. "Because I'm going to sacrifice him to summon Mefist the Infernal General!"

A wicked-looking warrior in armor appeared

on the field, riding on an armored horse. His attack points flashed: 1,800.

But Jaden smiled calmly. "Not bad," he told Chazz.

"Not bad?" Chazz couldn't believe Jaden's attitude. "You're something else, slacker, you know that? Acting all confident. But your lousy monsters won't get you out of this jam!"

· CHAPTER TWELVE ·

DUEL INTERRUPTED

Jaden looked at the cards in his hand, thoughtful. There had to be a way out of this. . . .

He heard a soft squeal and saw the Winged Kuriboh card glowing slightly. Jaden smiled.

"I know he's wrong, Kuriboh," he whispered. "'Cause Chazz doesn't know that my monsters and I . . . we have a bond."

Kuriboh winked, and Jaden looked over

his cards once again. Suddenly, he knew just what to do.

Then Alexis ran out onto the field.

"Guys, we got company!" she said. "Campus security. If they find us all in here, we'll get seriously busted!"

"Why?" Jaden asked. "We're all students here."

"The rules say no off-hour arena duels," Alexis replied. "Chazz knows that, but let me guess — he didn't tell you."

Chazz's two Obelisk friends were pulling him away from the field.

"Come on, let's go!" one urged, clearly worried.

"Well, it looks like you lucked out this time, slacker," Chazz told Jaden.

"What are you talking about? The match isn't over!" Jaden protested.

"Yeah, it is," Chazz said. "I've seen what I came to see. You're a sorry Duelist. Your beating Dr. Crowler was just a fluke."

Syrus yanked on Jaden's sleeve. "Come on, we've got to get out of here."

Jaden didn't want to move. The duel couldn't be finished! They couldn't stop now. But the serious look on Alexis's face convinced him.

"There'll be big trouble if we're caught," she warned.

Jaden nodded, and the three turned and ran to the entrance. Glancing over his shoulder, Jaden saw the figures of three security guards about to enter from the other side.

The friends emerged into the night air just in time. Jaden kicked at the dirt, frustrated.

"This stinks! I had that guy on the ropes!" he complained.

Alexis shook her head. "You certainly are stubborn, Jaden."

"Only about my dueling," Jaden told her.

Syrus shyly looked at the ground. "Thanks for getting us out in time," he said.

"Sure," Alexis replied. She turned to Jaden. "I'm just sorry you didn't get to finish your match with Chazz."

"It's okay! I know how it would have ended anyway," Jaden said.

Alexis raised an eyebrow. "Really?" she asked. "No offense, but from my point of view, it looked like you were in a pretty tight spot when you guys stopped."

"No way!" Jaden said. "Not after I drew this."

Jaden showed Alexis the next card in his

hand. "Monster Reborn," he said. "I would have used it to summon Wingman from the grave-yard."

In his mind, Jaden saw how the duel would have ended. Wingman diving to attack Mefist the Infernal General. The armored warrior crumbling under the power of Wingman's attack. Chazz's life points draining to zero . . .

Alexis's eyes widened. She was envisioning the move, too.

Jaden shrugged. "See ya!" he said. Then he ran off toward the Slifer Red dorm.

"Hey, wait up!" Syrus cried behind him.

But Jaden didn't slow down. He couldn't wait to get to sleep. Tomorrow was a new day — and the possibility of a new duel.

This was going to be one awesome year!